The HAUNTED LIBRARY

P9-DNF-853

FOR ALL MY NEW
SEATTLE FRIENDS

**AND THANK YOU, WLMA, FOR CREATING
THE OTTER AWARD FOR TRANSITIONAL READERS
AND FOR PUTTING HAUNTED LIBRARY #1
ON THE FIRST LIST!
—DHB**

* * * * * * * * * * * * * * *

GROSSET & DUNLAP
**Penguin Young Readers Group
An Imprint of Penguin Random House LLC**

If you purchased this book without a cover, you should be aware that this book is stolen property. It was reported as "unsold and destroyed" to the publisher, and neither the author nor the publisher has received any payment for this "stripped book."

Penguin supports copyright. Copyright fuels creativity, encourages diverse voices, promotes free speech, and creates a vibrant culture. Thank you for buying an authorized edition of this book and for complying with copyright laws by not reproducing, scanning, or distributing any part of it in any form without permission. You are supporting writers and allowing Penguin to continue to publish books for every reader.

Text copyright © 2017 by Dori Hillestad Butler. Illustrations copyright © 2017 by Aurore Damant. All rights reserved. Published by Grosset & Dunlap, an imprint of Penguin Random House LLC, 345 Hudson Street, New York, New York 10014. GROSSET & DUNLAP is a trademark of Penguin Random House LLC. Printed in the USA.

Library of Congress Cataloging-in-Publication Data is available.

ISBN 9780515157116   10 9 8 7 6 5 4 3 2

The HAUNTED LIBRARY

THE UNDERGROUND GHOSTS

SUPER SPECIAL

BY DORI HILLESTAD BUTLER
ILLUSTRATED BY AURORE DAMANT

GROSSET & DUNLAP * AN IMPRINT OF PENGUIN RANDOM HOUSE

GHOSTLY GLOSSARY

EXPAND
When ghosts make themselves larger

GLOW
What ghosts do so humans can see them

HAUNT
Where ghosts live

PASS THROUGH
When ghosts travel through walls, doors, and other solid objects

SHRINK
When ghosts make themselves smaller

SKIZZY
When ghosts feel sick to their stomachs

SOLIDS
What ghosts call humans

SPEW
Ghostly vomit

SWIM
When ghosts move freely through the air

TRANSFORMATION
When a ghost takes a solid object and turns it into a ghostly object

WAIL
What ghosts do so humans can hear them

CHAPTER 1

A VISIT TO SEATTLE

ook, Kaz!" Little John gazed out Claire's window. "We're up above the clouds!"

Kaz didn't want to look. He, Little John, and Claire were on an airplane. Claire had flown on an airplane before, but this was a new experience for the ghosts. Kaz wasn't sure he liked it.

"I wonder what it would feel like to pass through a cloud," Little John said, edging closer to the window.

Kaz pulled him back. "We're not going to find out," he said.

Claire smiled at Kaz and Little John as they floated above her. She couldn't talk to them because there were too many people around. Those people couldn't see or hear ghosts like she could, so they would wonder who she was talking to.

Claire and her ghost friends were on their way to Seattle. Claire's parents were at a convention for detectives, and Grandma Karen was at a convention for librarians. So they had arranged for Claire to spend the week with her aunt Beth and cousin Maddie.

Back before she met Kaz and Little John, Claire used to live in Seattle. She saw Aunt Beth and Maddie all the time then because they took care of her whenever her parents were away. But

Claire's family had moved to Iowa last year to be closer to Grandma Karen. This was Claire's first trip back to Seattle. And her first trip without her parents.

Claire couldn't imagine a better time to visit Aunt Beth and Maddie because Halloween was this Friday. Maddie was on the teen advisory board at the Seattle Public Library, and they had planned an overnight Halloween party at the library. There would be ghost stories, crafts, and games. Claire could hardly wait.

"Remember, Little John. You said you'd be on your best behavior if you got to come to Seattle with Claire and me," Kaz said.

"I *am* on my best behavior," Little John replied.

"No glowing. No wailing. And no scaring solid people," Kaz said. "No passing through airplane windows, either!"

"I was just looking out the window,"
Little John said. "I wasn't going to pass
through it. Relax, Kaz. We're on vacation!"

How was Kaz supposed to relax when
he had to worry about his little brother?
Honestly, Kaz was surprised Mom and

Pops let him and Little John go all the way to Seattle. Especially after everything that had happened to their family.

A year ago, Kaz and Little John lived with their big brother, Finn, their parents, their grandparents, and their dog, Cosmo, in an old abandoned schoolhouse. Everything was fine until Finn accidentally passed through the schoolhouse wall, and the wind blew him away.

Grandmom and Grandpop tried to rescue Finn, but they blew away, too.

A few months after that, the schoolhouse was torn down and the rest of the ghosts blew away. Kaz didn't think he'd ever see his family again.

The wind blew Kaz to a small-town library. That was where he met Claire. Claire lived above the library with her parents and her grandma.

Kaz and Claire had formed a detective agency, C & K Ghost Detectives, to solve ghostly mysteries and find Kaz's family. It took a while, but they found everyone—Kaz's whole family.

Now what if someone got lost again? What if Kaz or Little John got lost in Seattle?

"This airplane is kind of like a water bottle for solid people," Little John said as a flight attendant moved through the aisle and collected trash.

"How do you figure that?" Kaz asked.

"If solid people want to go somewhere, they travel inside an airplane," Little John said. "If we want to go somewhere, we travel in there." He pointed at the empty water bottle on the tray table in front of Claire.

Kaz couldn't argue with that.

A voice came over the loudspeaker: "In preparation for landing, please make sure your seat backs and tray tables are in their full upright and locked positions."

"We better go back inside Claire's water bottle," Kaz said to his brother.

"Aw. Do we have to?" Little John asked.

"Yes," Kaz replied. The ghosts shrank down . . . down . . . down . . . and passed through the side of the bottle.

Claire held her water bottle between her knees while she lifted her tray table and clipped it into the back of the seat in front of her.

"Hey!" Little John called to Claire. "We want to see out the window."

"Speak for yourself," Kaz moaned. Looking out the window made him feel skizzy.

But Claire raised her water bottle to the window, anyway.

"Thanks, Claire," Little John said. "If you don't want to see, Kaz, close your eyes."

So Kaz closed his eyes. He didn't open them until the plane was safely on the ground.

* * * * * * * * * * * * * * *

Since Claire was traveling without an adult, a flight attendant walked her through the busy airport. Kaz and Little John remained inside the bottle.

"There she is! There's Claire!" A teenage girl with bright red hair waved eagerly. The lady beside her waved, too.

Claire grinned. "That's my cousin and my aunt," she told the flight attendant. Rolling her suitcase behind her, she ran

to the red-haired teenager and lady, and threw an arm around each of them. "Hi, Maddie! Hi, Aunt Beth!"

"Oh, it's so good to see you again, honey," Aunt Beth said, hugging her back. She glanced at the flight attendant. "Thanks for looking out for my niece."

"My pleasure," the flight attendant replied. She waved goodbye and hurried away.

"How was the flight?" Aunt Beth asked Claire as they headed for the parking garage.

"Good," Claire replied.

They took an elevator down to the second floor of the parking garage and walked over to a blue car. Maddie put Claire's suitcase in the trunk. She started to open the front door, but then got into the backseat instead. "I don't get to see Claire very often, so I'm going to sit in back with her," she told her mom.

"I'm sure Claire would like that," Aunt Beth said.

Claire nodded. She held her water bottle on her lap while she buckled her seatbelt.

Aunt Beth started the car and drove out of the parking garage.

"Hey, Mom," Maddie said, leaning forward in her seat. "Can I have the week off from homeschool to hang out with Claire?"

"No," Aunt Beth said. She sounded surprised that Maddie would even ask. "Claire probably has work from her school that she has to do while she's here."

"I do," Claire said.

"Good. If you spend your mornings on schoolwork, you can have the afternoons to do whatever you'd like. What *would* you like to do while you're here, Claire?" Aunt Beth smiled at Claire in the rearview mirror.

Claire shrugged. "I don't know. Mostly just hang out with you guys. And go to the Halloween party at the library. I'm looking forward to that!"

"Unfortunately, there may not be a Halloween party," Maddie said glumly.

"What?" Claire asked. "Why not?"

"Some weird stuff has been happening at the library," Maddie said. "Kids aren't signing up for the party because they think the library's haunted. Remember before you moved, you told people you could see ghosts? I know I didn't believe you then, but . . . were you telling the truth?"

"Maddie," Aunt Beth laughed. "You're fourteen years old. You know there's no such thing as ghosts."

Little John clucked his tongue. "There . . . is . . . *too* . . . such . . . thing . . . as . . . ghosts . . . ," he wailed inside the bottle.

"Little John!" Kaz scolded. He clapped his hand over his brother's mouth.

Maddie drew in her breath. "What was that?" She peered at Claire's water bottle. She heard Little John, but she couldn't see him.

Even Aunt Beth turned to look. "That was a funny voice, Claire," she said.

"No wailing! Remember?" Kaz said to his brother.

Little John lowered his eyes. "Sorry. But I don't like it when people say there's no such thing as ghosts."

Aunt Beth turned her attention back to the road.

Maddie elbowed Claire. "What *was* that?" she asked again.

Claire glanced down at her ghost friends.

"Should I wail some more?" Little John asked Kaz.

"No!" Kaz said.

Claire leaned toward her cousin. "Can I tell you a secret?" she whispered.

"Of course." Maddie looked at Claire curiously.

"I *was* telling the truth when I said I could see ghosts," Claire whispered. "In fact, I brought two ghost friends with me. They're in here." She picked up her water bottle. "That's what you heard just now."

"They're in there?" Maddie's eyes opened wide. "They must be awfully small," she said in a low voice.

"They can shrink and expand," Claire whispered.

"I wish I could see them," Maddie whispered back.

"What are you girls whispering about back there?" Aunt Beth asked.

"Nothing," Maddie said loudly. "Better not tell my mom," she whispered to Claire. "She'll never believe you."

Claire nodded. "Most people don't," she said softly. "I'm used to it."

CHAPTER 2

MEET LITTLE JOHN

So tell me what's been happening at the library," Claire said later when she and Maddie were setting up a cot next to Maddie's bed. Kaz and Little John hovered above them. "You said kids weren't signing up for the Halloween party because they think the library's haunted."

"It *is* haunted," Maddie said. She handed Claire two pillows.

"How do you know?" Claire asked.

She plopped down on the cot and grabbed her notebook and pen. "Have you seen a ghost in the library?"

"No, but I've heard it," Maddie said. "So have a bunch of other people. It lives inside the dumbwaiter."

"What's a dumbwaiter?" Little John asked Kaz.

Kaz shrugged.

"What's a dumbwaiter?" Claire asked Maddie.

"It's like an elevator for books instead of people," Maddie replied. "There's a little compartment, and librarians put books in there and send them to people who want them on other floors in the library."

"Hmm, okay," Claire said. She wrote *Seattle Public Library Ghost* in big letters in her notebook. Below that, she wrote *lives*

in the dumbwaiter. "So, is that where you hear the ghost? Inside the dumbwaiter?"

"Yes," Maddie said.

"What does it say?" Claire asked.

"It doesn't say anything," Maddie replied. "It just cries and cries and cries. It's a very sad ghost." She sat down on her own bed across from Claire.

"What makes her so sure it's a ghost?" Kaz asked. So many of the cases C & K Ghost Detectives had solved ended up not being ghosts.

Claire wrote *sad ghost* and *cries a lot.* "How do you know it's a ghost?" she asked.

"What else could it be?" Maddie asked. "People always think a real kid got stuck in the dumbwaiter—"

"Ghost kids *are* real kids!" Little John blurted.

"Shh!" Kaz said. He couldn't hear Maddie over Little John.

"So they get a librarian to come open it up, but there's never anyone in there," Maddie went on. "The crying gets louder, though, when the dumbwaiter is open. Plus, there are all these other weird things that keep happening at the library. Elevators and escalators stop working for no reason. Doors open and close all by themselves. It's got to be a ghost, don't you think?"

"Maybe," Claire said. She wrote down everything her cousin said.

"If you can see and talk to the ghost, maybe you can find out why it's so sad,"

Maddie said. "If we fix whatever's wrong, maybe it'll go away. Then kids will sign up for the Halloween party, and we won't have to cancel it."

"I'll do my best," Claire said, closing her notebook.

"Good. We'll go to the library tomorrow. As soon as Mom says we've done enough schoolwork," Maddie said. She picked up Claire's water bottle and tried to see inside. "I can't believe your ghost friends can really fit in there."

"Oh, they're not in there right now," Claire said.

"They're not?" Maddie said. "Where are they?"

"We're . . . over . . . here . . . ," Little John wailed. "Behind you . . ." He started to glow.

Maddie turned. She opened her mouth, but no words came out.

24

"Maddie, meet Little John," Claire said, gesturing toward him.

"Hi . . . ," Little John wailed. He waved at Maddie.

Maddie grinned. "Hey, I can see ghosts now, too! Just like you."

"You can only see him because he's glowing," Claire said. "That's what ghosts do when they want us to see them. My other ghost friend, Kaz, can't glow."

"Don't remind me," Kaz moaned. It was the only ghost skill he hadn't learned yet.

"But he's here, too," Claire said. "Kaz, say hello to Maddie."

"Hello . . . ," Kaz wailed. He tried to glow. He closed his eyes and clenched his fists and told his body to glow. But as usual, nothing happened.

"Hi," Maddie said.

Little John stopped glowing.

Maddie blinked. "Hey, where'd that ghost go?" she asked.

"He's still there," Claire said. "It takes a lot of energy for ghosts to glow, so he's not glowing anymore."

"You mean he's tired?" Maddie asked.

"Sort of," Claire replied, stifling a yawn. "Ghosts don't sleep. But they run out of energy if they use their ghost skills a lot."

"Speaking of sleep," Maddie said. "You look like you could use some."

"I am tired," Claire admitted. "It's two hours later in Iowa than it is here."

"Oh, that's right," Maddie said, leaping up from her bed. "You should go to sleep. I think I'll go watch TV with my mom. See you in the morning."

"See you in the morning," Claire said, snuggling down under her covers.

* * * * * * * * * * * * * * * *

"Wow," Little John said from inside Claire's water bottle. "Have you ever seen such tall buildings before, Kaz?"

It was Tuesday afternoon, and Claire and Maddie were on a city bus headed for the library.

"No," Kaz replied. "But we've never been in such a big city before." Seattle was way bigger than their town in Iowa.

The bus made a wide turn into an underground passageway. It continued through a narrow concrete tunnel, which eventually led to a large underground platform. A sign on the wall said WESTLAKE CENTER.

"Are we getting off here?" Claire asked Maddie as the bus slowed to a stop. A bunch of people around them stood up.

"No. Next stop," Maddie replied.

The bus lurched forward, picking up speed as it moved into another tunnel. Just then, two ghostly figures, a man and a woman, passed through the front of the bus.

"Who are they?" Kaz asked as the other ghosts sailed over Claire's head.

Claire turned all the way around in her seat and stared.

Little John passed through Claire's water bottle. "Hello?" he called to the other ghosts.

"Get back in here, Little John," Kaz ordered. "Claire and Maddie are getting off at the next stop."

Little John exp-a-a-a-a-nded to full size and followed the other ghosts.

"LITTLE JOHN!" Kaz yelled. He passed through the bottle and hurried after his brother.

The bus stopped at another underground platform. The girls stood up and started making their way down the aisle. Claire glanced nervously over her shoulder as the other ghosts passed through the back of the bus.

"No! Come back, ghosts!" Little John cried, hovering in place.

"Hurry, Little John," Kaz said. "We have to get back in the bottle." Claire was already at the front of the bus.

"Go on, girls," the bus driver said. "I've got a schedule to keep."

Maddie gave Claire a nudge, and the girls stepped off the bus, leaving Kaz and Little John behind.

Not knowing what to do, Kaz grabbed Little John's suspenders and pulled him up through the top of the bus just before it sped away.

"Oh, good. Now we can find those other ghosts," Little John said, looking all around.

But the other ghosts were gone.

"We need to find Claire," Kaz said. He scanned the platform. He didn't see Claire anywhere in the crowd.

Fortunately, he heard her: "Kaz? Where are you, Kaz?"

"Where are *you*, Claire?" Kaz called back.

"Over here. By the wall," Claire replied.

Kaz grabbed Little John's hand and followed Claire's voice.

"There they are!" Little John pointed at two girls who were leaning against the wall.

Kaz and Little John dived down and passed through the side of Claire's water bottle.

"Oh, good!" Claire said. She hugged her bottle as though she were hugging the ghosts.

"I take it your ghost friends are back?" Maddie said.

"Yes," Claire said.

But even though they were safe inside Claire's water bottle, Kaz's heart went *Thump! Thump! Thump! Thump!* "You can't go swimming off like that, Little John," he cried.

"I just wanted to meet those other ghosts," Little John said.

"We have to stick with Claire," Kaz said. "We don't want to get lost in Seattle."

"You're not being very fun, Kaz," Little John grumbled.

"And you're not being very careful," Kaz said.

What were Mom and Pops *thinking* when they said Little John could come to Seattle with him and Claire? Little John was an accident waiting to happen.

CHAPTER 3

ANOTHER HAUNTED LIBRARY

s *that* the library?" Little John asked from inside Claire's water bottle. The Seattle Public Library didn't look like any other building the ghosts had ever seen before. It was all glass, and parts of it stuck out in weird shapes and angles.

"Must be," Kaz said as Claire and Maddie went inside. "Wow. This place is huge!"

There was a bright yellow escalator

in front of them. Three elevators slightly to the left. A long checkout desk to the right. And rows of bookshelves beyond the checkout desk.

Kaz also noticed a strange machine that carried books from the outside book drop, up some sort of conveyor belt that disappeared through an opening in the ceiling.

"Does Andrea still work here?" Claire asked Maddie as they walked over to the elevators. "She was my favorite librarian."

"Andrea is everyone's favorite librarian," Maddie said. "You want to go say hi to her before we visit the ghost?"

Claire nodded eagerly.

"Okay. We can find out if any more kids have signed up for the Halloween

party while we're there, too," Maddie said.

The girls walked past a table where a lady security guard sat watching three computer screens, then continued around a glass wall that said CHILDREN'S CENTER in purple letters.

"Wow! Look at all the books," Kaz said. There were more books in this room than there were in their whole library back home.

"Look at all the toys!" Little John stared at a large play area behind a desk where two librarians sat. A group of solid boys and girls played at a table with a large train set. Others were spread out around the floor with puzzles and blocks. Parents and grandparents sat on benches around them.

Before Kaz could stop him, Little John passed through the bottle. He exp-a-a-a-a-a-nded, then wafted over to the play area.

"Now what are you doing?" Kaz asked. He passed through the bottle and exp-a-a-a-a-a-nded, too.

"Just looking around," Little John replied.

Kaz drifted up above the desk, where he could keep an eye on Little John *and* on Claire and Maddie.

"Hi, Andrea," Claire said to the dark-haired librarian at the desk.

The librarian looked up. "Oh my goodness!" she said with a big smile. She turned to the other librarian. "Do you know who this is, Lynette?"

"No," the other librarian said, barely looking up from her magazine.

"This is Claire Kendall," Andrea said. "She always attended our programs, but she moved away a year or so ago. Are you back, Claire?"

"Just for a visit," Claire said. "I'll be here for the Halloween party!"

"Oh good," Andrea said.

Lynette scowled. "We've never had an overnight party in the library

before," she said, turning the page in her magazine. "I don't know why we need to have one now."

Andrea looked surprised. "Because it's fun for the kids," she said. "Wouldn't you have enjoyed spending the night in the library when you were a kid?"

"Not really," Lynette said.

"Do we have enough people signed up for the party?" Maddie asked.

"I think so." Andrea rifled through some papers on her desk, found the one she wanted, and pulled it out. "We've got fifteen kids signed up. That's not a lot, but it's enough. The party's still three days away. Maybe we'll get a few more signed up by then."

"Yay!" Claire and Maddie slapped high fives.

"Guess that means I'll be working

Friday night," Lynette grumbled.

"Don't pay any attention to Lynette," Maddie whispered as she led Claire away from the desk. "I don't know why she's a children's librarian. I don't think she likes kids very much. Let's go find the ghost."

"Little John?" Kaz called as Claire and Maddie headed for the door. "We're leaving."

"I don't want to," Little John said, his eyes focused on a solid girl who was driving a train around the track. She had long dark braids, and she looked like she was around his age.

"You can't stay here by yourself," Kaz said, hands on his hips.

"Can . . . I . . . play . . . with . . . you . . . ?" Little John wailed at the girl with the braids.

Kaz gasped. "Little John! You did *not* just wail at that solid girl!"

Claire stopped in the doorway. She motioned for Maddie to stop, too. All the other solid children looked around. They couldn't see Little John, but they could hear him.

"I'm . . . right . . . here . . . ," Little John wailed some more. Then he started to glow.

"Little John!" Kaz cried. Now all the solid people could *see* his brother, too. If they were looking.

Claire and Maddie walked back over. "That's—" Maddie gasped. She pointed at Little John, but Claire grabbed Maddie's finger and made her stop pointing.

The girl with the braids grinned at Little John.

A boy who was building a tower on the floor screamed. His tower crashed to the floor as he scrambled to his feet and ran over to his mother.

"What's the matter, Jackson?" the mom asked. She held a baby in one arm and hugged Jackson with the other. She hadn't noticed Little John. Neither had any of the other adults.

Little John stopped glowing.

"I saw a ghost!" Jackson said.

"I don't see anything," Jackson's mom said, patting his back.

"Don't be scared," Claire said, walking over to Jackson.

"I heard something," said one of the other moms. "Someone said, 'I'm right here.'" She turned and frowned. "Quinn, was that you? Are you trying to scare little kids again?"

A boy in a striped shirt came out from behind one of the bookshelves. "No!" he said. He held a stack of chapter books in his hands.

"It's gone now," said the girl with the braids. "But Jackson's telling the truth. There was a ghost. I saw it, too."

"So did I," said another girl. "It was a boy and he was all blue, except you could see through him."

Kaz glared at Little John. Claire glanced at her ghost friends, unsure of what to do.

Little John shrank. "I just wanted to play with those kids," he said in a small voice.

"I don't know what you saw, but I promise you there are no ghosts in this library," Andrea said firmly from the desk.

"That's not a promise I would make," Lynette said in a mysterious voice.

"I heard there's a ghost on the fifth floor that cries," said a girl around Claire's age.

"I saw a ghost on the third floor once," said a light-haired boy. "He had chains and he was rattling them in people's faces."

"Really?" Maddie asked.

"I came here at night once to hear an author, and there was a ghost in the auditorium," said the first girl. "It flicked the lights and it made the microphone screech and it said in a really scary voice, 'Everyone . . . go . . . home.'"

A girl in a yellow sundress ran to the desk. "I changed my mind," she told Andrea. "I don't want to sign up for the Halloween party. I don't want to spend the night in a haunted library."

Two other kids ran over, too. "We don't, either," they said.

"Hold on," Maddie said to the kids. "You don't have to worry about ghosts. This is my cousin, Claire." She put her arm around Claire. "She can see and talk to ghosts!"

Claire looked a little alarmed as everyone in the children's center stared at her.

"She's going to go talk to the library ghost and get it to leave," Maddie went on. "You don't have to be afraid to come to the Halloween party. Right, Claire?"

"Right," Claire said uneasily.

"I don't know," Lynette said. "If a ghost doesn't want to leave, I doubt there's anything a little girl like her can do to make it go away."

CHAPTER 4

THE DUMBWAITER

Did you hear that?" Claire sputtered as the girls walked over to the elevators. "That other librarian called me a *little* girl!"

Kaz and Little John hurried to catch up.

"Like I said, I don't know why Lynette is a children's librarian," Maddie said. "She's good with books and technology, but she's not so good with kids. I think she's *scared* of kids."

Claire looked doubtful. "Grown-ups

aren't scared of kids," she said.

"Some of them are," Maddie said.

The elevator doors opened, and Claire and Maddie stepped inside. Kaz and Little John followed them in.

"Which floor?" Claire asked.

"Fifth. That's where the dumbwaiter is," Maddie said. She reached around Claire and pushed the button. The doors closed, and the elevator started rising.

"Wow. There are eleven floors in this library," Little John said, staring at all the elevator buttons.

"That's a lot of floors," Kaz said. He wondered what was on all those floors.

The elevator stopped on the fifth floor. The doors opened, and everyone got out.

"Where's the dumbwaiter?" Claire asked.

There was a railing in front of them.

Beyond the railing was a huge wall of light blue diamond-shaped windows.

"Over here," Maddie said. She led Claire and the ghosts around the corner.

There were no bookshelves on this floor. Just lots of people working at computers.

"This is it," Maddie said. She stopped in front of a tall pillar that had a metal door in the middle. The door was closed.

Claire put her ear to the door. "I don't hear anything," she said.

"Just wait," Maddie said. "You will."

The girls and the ghosts watched the door and waited for something to happen.

"The ghost is going to start crying any second now," Maddie said, shifting her weight from one foot to the other.

They waited some more.

Finally, Little John said, "What are we

waiting for? Let's go in there and talk to the ghost."

"Oh, that's a good idea," Claire said.

"What's a good idea?" Maddie asked.

"Little John wants to go inside the dumbwaiter and talk to the ghost," Claire told Maddie.

"I don't know if we should barge in uninvited," Kaz said. "Let's just talk to it from out here." He wafted over to the door. "Hello? Is anyone in there?"

No one answered.

"We're ghosts, too," Little John said. "Any ghost in there will be happy to see us." He shrank a little so he'd fit inside the compartment, then plunged headfirst through the door.

Kaz wasn't so sure the ghost would be happy to see them. But he shrank and followed his brother, anyway.

There were two shelves inside the
dumbwaiter. Kaz and Little John checked
both shelves. There was nothing on either
one. No books. No other ghosts. Nothing.

"Maybe the ghost isn't home right
now," Little John said. "Should we wait?"

"Nah," Kaz said. "Let's go report back to
Claire." They passed through the door and
exp-a-a-a-a-a-nded.

"There's no ghost in there," Little John
announced.

"They said there isn't a ghost in there," Claire told Maddie.

"There has to be," Maddie said, staring at the pillar. "People hear it crying in there all the time."

"Maybe it left," Claire said with a shrug.

"Maybe," Maddie said. But it didn't sound like she believed that.

"Or maybe it's not a real ghost," Kaz said. "Maybe it's just someone pretending to be a ghost to make people think the library is haunted when it's really not."

"Solid people like to do that sort of thing," Little John said.

"Especially around Halloween," Kaz added. He felt bad that Maddie couldn't hear what he and Little John were saying. But if they wailed, then *everyone* in the library would hear them.

"Let's search the rest of the library,"

Maddie said. "Maybe it found a new place to hang out." She led Claire past the computers and over to a tall, narrow escalator. Behind the escalator was a staircase that led down into a strange red tunnel. Kaz hoped they weren't going down there.

"Should we split up?" Claire asked. "We could cover more ground in less time."

"Well, I can't see ghosts like you can," Maddie reminded Claire.

"I don't mean *you and I* should split up. I mean Kaz, Little John, and I should split up," Claire said.

"What?" Kaz cried. He didn't like that idea. He didn't like it at all.

"I know there are places in the library that we can't search," Claire said to Maddie. "But Kaz and Little John can because no one will see them."

"Yeah, like the second floor," Maddie said. "That's where people who work here sort books. We can't go there. We can't go in the offices on the third floor or the eleventh floor, either. You have to be a librarian to get into any of those places."

"I want to search the special places where only librarians can go!" Little John exclaimed.

"Okay, Little John. Look over there, past the railing." Claire pointed across the room. "See how there aren't any walls over there? That part of the library is open from the third floor all the way to the top. If you swim to the top, you should be able to pass through the windows and go into the offices on the eleventh floor."

"Have him search the ninth and tenth floors, too," Maddie said. "You and I can search the book spiral. And your other

ghost friend can go down there." She pointed down the stairs. The stairs that led into the strange red tunnel.

"Down *there*?" Kaz cried.

"He can search the fourth, third, second, and first floors," Maddie said. "Tell him to pay extra attention to the second floor, since we can't go there."

"He can hear you," Claire said.

"Meet you back in the children's center," Little John said, swimming away.

"Okay," Claire said.

"Wait! What's down there?" Kaz asked. He peered down at the tunnel.

"That's the fourth floor. It's just meeting rooms. No big deal," Claire said. She stepped onto the narrow escalator.

No big deal, huh, Kaz thought. Claire wouldn't lie to him. So he took a deep breath and floated slowly down the stairs.

CHAPTER 5

SEARCHING FOR GHOSTS

The fourth floor was creepy. There were no outside windows. Not where Kaz was, anyway. No bookshelves, either. Just a narrow, dimly lit hallway that circled the floor. The walls, floor, and ceiling were all painted a deep, dark red.

"Hello? Are there any other ghosts on this floor?" Kaz called as he drifted in and out of meeting rooms.

He didn't see any ghosts on the fourth floor.

He came to another set of stairs and swam down to the third floor. This floor was a lot brighter than the fourth floor. The ceiling and slanted glass walls went up, up, up to the top floor of the library.

There was another outside entrance to the library on this floor. And another checkout desk . . . an information desk . . . bookshelves . . . a store that sold cards and bags and a bunch of other stuff . . . a planter with real plants . . . and lots of places for solid people to sit and read.

Words on a concrete wall told Kaz he was in a living room. There was a living room in the library back home, but that one was just for Claire and her family. It was in their apartment above the library. This living room looked like it was for everyone.

Kaz wafted past the living room, through a section marked Teen Area, and up over a wall. There were several librarians working at desks back here.

But no ghosts.

Kaz went all the way to the end of the office area and returned to the main part of the library. He wafted past the checkout desk and saw a bright yellow escalator going down. He followed it, expecting to come out on the second floor.

But somehow he was back on the first floor now. The door where they had come in was right in front of him. The elevators and children's center were to his right. And the checkout and returns were to his left. *Where is the second floor?* Kaz wondered.

Well, he hadn't searched this floor yet. Maybe he'd find another escalator that

led to the second floor somewhere on this floor.

He continued past the checkout and returns area . . . past the reserves . . . and into the world languages area. There was writing on the wood floor here. Kaz couldn't read any of it because it was written backward. Some of it was even in other languages.

He drifted in and out of small storage rooms, in and out of restrooms, and through a dark auditorium beside the children's center.

Still no ghosts. No secret escalator to the second floor, either.

Kaz glanced over at the checkout and returns area. He stared at the strange machine that carried books up through an opening in the ceiling.

Wait. Maddie said that books were

sorted on the second floor. Maybe you could get to the second floor by following that machine.

Kaz swam over. He sailed up, up, up along the conveyor belt and through the ceiling.

Aha! *This* was a new part of the library. This must be the second floor.

Kaz watched books move along several conveyor belts. Sometimes the books fell into bins. Sometimes they rode the conveyor belt to another bin. *How do the books know where to go?* Kaz wondered.

There were several solid people in here who watched computer screens, pushed buttons on machines, and wheeled carts in and out of the room. Kaz followed one of those people to some sort of loading area. There was a big garage door that was open to the Outside. Kaz quickly

backstroked out of there. He didn't want to get blown into the Outside.

He searched the rest of the second floor. There were no ghosts here, either.

* * * * * * * * * * * * * * * * *

"Hi, Kaz!" Little John waved from the back of the children's center. "Did you find any ghosts?"

"No," Kaz replied. "Did you?"

"No. But I found a secret room," Little John said. "It's in there." He pointed at a slanted mustard-colored wall below him.

Kaz hadn't noticed that room before. But as he wafted over, he realized it wasn't totally secret. Not like the secret room in the library back home. Solid people could go inside this room, if they saw the entrance.

"Did you go in?" Kaz asked his

brother. "Are there any ghosts in there?"

"I went in. There was a lady reading a Halloween book to a bunch of solid kids in there. But there weren't any ghosts," Little John replied.

Claire and Maddie came back a few minutes later. Solid children surrounded them as soon as they walked in. "Did you find the ghost? Did you find the ghost?"

One of those children zoomed right through Kaz.

"Ack!" Kaz shrieked. He didn't like it when solid people passed through him.

"No," Claire said. She raised an eyebrow at Kaz and Little John to see whether they had found any ghosts. They both shook their heads.

"We've searched this whole library," Claire said to the other kids. "Any ghosts that were here before are gone now."

"That's right," Maddie said. "So come to the Halloween party. There's—"
A strange clanging noise cut her off.

"What was *that*?" a girl asked, her eyes wide.

"Sounds like our ghost is back," Lynette said.

Andrea nudged Lynette. "Careful," she said. "We don't want to scare the children."

CREEAAAAAK! CREAK! CLANG!

"I bet it's the ghost with the chains," said the light-haired boy.

"Mommy, I'm scared," said a young boy. He raised his arms, and a woman picked him up.

"It sounds like it's coming from upstairs. Let's go check it out," Maddie said to Claire. The girls raced for the escalator. Kaz and Little John followed close behind.

But when they got about halfway up, the escalator suddenly stopped. Kaz and Little John hovered in place behind Claire and Maddie.

"What happened? Why did we stop?" Claire asked, looking down at her feet.

"I bet the ghost made the escalator stop working," Maddie said. "He's done that before."

Kaz didn't know how a ghost could

make an escalator stop working. But maybe if he spent more time around escalators, he would know.

The girls scrambled up the rest of the escalator stairs, and the ghosts swam behind them. When they reached the third floor, they saw a crowd gathered near the big planter. Everyone stared up at the angled glass ceiling.

"What's going on?" Claire asked from the back of the crowd.

CLANG! CLANG! CLANG!

An older boy in front of Claire pointed. "They're washing the windows."

The ghosts swam up to get a closer look at the two solid men who dangled from ropes outside the building.

"That looks dangerous for solid people," Little John said.

"Yeah, so don't glow!" Kaz warned.

"You don't want to scare them and make them fall."

The men on the other side of the glass were holding hoses and squeegees. Large hooks that were attached to their ropes clanged against the glass. *That's* what made the strange noise, not a ghost.

Kaz and Little John floated back down to Claire and Maddie.

"I guess you're right, Claire," Maddie said as they moved away from the crowd. "The ghost is gone. Should we go back to my house?"

"Sure," Claire said.

Kaz and Little John shrank down . . . down . . . down . . . and swam into Claire's water bottle. Then they all left the library.

"Do you mind if we stop at Pike Place

and get some flowers for my mom?" Maddie asked. "Her birthday was last week and I never got her a gift."

"Sure. I love the market," Claire replied. They walked down a very steep hill, crossed a couple of busy streets, then walked into a crowded open market.

"Fresh fish!" a man behind the counter yelled. He tossed a large package into the crowd.

A woman stepped up and caught it with both hands.

"Do you want to see a really weird fish?" Maddie asked. She grabbed Claire's hand and wove through the crowd. Kaz and Little John stayed inside the bottle.

When they reached the case, Maddie pointed at a large fish with a wide, gaping mouth. It was right at Kaz and Little John's eye level, and it looked big enough to swallow them whole—if it was still alive.

A little sign stuck in the ice said LOOK OUT! I'M A MONKFISH!

Without warning, the monkfish popped up and LUNGED toward the ghosts. "AAAHHHHHHH!" they both screamed.

t's alive!" a younger boy cried as Claire and Maddie leaped back from the monkfish.

"It is not," said an older boy beside him.

"It is too," the younger boy insisted.

The monkfish just lay there on the ice now. It didn't *look* like it was alive. But Kaz couldn't tell for sure.

"Can I help whoever's next?" asked the man behind the counter. He wore

a white apron and a name badge that
said BILL.

The fish popped up again.

"AAAHHHHHHH!" Kaz and Little
John grabbed on to each other inside the
bottle. The solid people standing near the
glass case shrieked.

"*Is* it alive?" the younger boy asked
Bill.

"Is what alive?" Bill asked. "Oh. This
fish? This one right here?" He poked it

with his finger. "It feels dead. Would you like to touch it?"

"No way!" the boy shrieked.

Bill smiled. "Or maybe it *is* still alive." The fish popped up again. But this time Bill let the crowd see that there was a stick attached to the back of the fish. He used the stick to make the fish pop up.

A bunch of people laughed.

"Told you it wasn't alive," the older boy behind Claire and Maddie said to the younger boy. "That guy's just playing a Halloween trick on everyone."

"He does that even when it's not Halloween. I think he likes scaring the tourists," Maddie said as she and Claire moved away from the counter. "Come on. Let's get some flowers."

The girls strolled past long tables of flower bouquets. Maddie chose one

with a mix of large blue, yellow, and white flowers. Then they left the market.

They dashed down several flights of stairs to reach the underground transit station. A bus waited at the other end of the platform.

"That's our bus," Maddie said, running toward it. She and Claire got on, paid their fares, and sat down on the first open seat. The ghosts stayed inside the bottle.

"Do you think we'll see those ghosts that we saw this morning?" Little John asked as the bus sped through a tunnel.

"I don't know," Kaz said.

They kept their eyes open, but no ghosts passed through the bus this time.

* * * * * * * * * * * * * * *

That night, Aunt Beth made spaghetti for dinner.

"I love spaghetti," Claire said. She plopped a large serving of noodles onto her plate. Kaz and Little John hovered above the table.

"I like the noodles, but not the sauce," Maddie said. "I'm a vegetarian, but Mom still tries to sneak hamburger in the sauce."

"You need protein, Maddie," Aunt Beth said.

"You can get protein without eating meat," Maddie said. "Hey, Claire. The teen advisory board is going to have touch-and-feel boxes at the Halloween party. What do you think? Should we put cold spaghetti in one of them? We could tell kids it's intestines. Or maybe brains."

"Sure," Claire said with a laugh.

Aunt Beth reached for a slice of garlic bread. "What else are you going to put in them?" she asked.

"Peeled grapes," Maddie said. "Those will be eyeballs. Unpopped popcorn will be monster teeth. Sliced bananas will be witch's tongues. Oh! We also talked

about putting a box over a hole in the table and having one of us sit under it. When a kid puts their hand in that box, the person under the table will reach through the hole and grab the kid's hand!"

Aunt Beth gasped.

"Now, *that's* scary," Claire said.

"Too scary?" Maddie asked.

"I don't know," Claire said, wiping her mouth. "Maybe."

"Some kids like to be scared, though," Maddie said. "Especially on Halloween."

"Oh! We can scare them. Can't we, Kaz?" Little John said. "We can glow and wail at the party. Should I tell Maddie that?"

"No," Kaz said. "No glowing or wailing, remember?"

"Not even on Halloween?" Little John asked.

"Not even on Halloween," Kaz said.

"But you heard Maddie. Some kids want to be scared. They might want to see a real, live ghost on Halloween," Little John argued.

"NO!" Kaz said again. "How many times do I have to say it? NO! NO! NO! NO! NO!"

* * * * * * * * * * * * * * *

That night, Claire and Maddie stayed up to watch scary movies. Kaz and Little John watched, too.

"Look at that ghost riding in the car with the top down." Little John pointed at the TV. "That wouldn't really happen. The ghost would blow away."

"I know!" Kaz laughed. "I don't think moviemakers know anything about ghosts. Do you, Claire?"

But Claire didn't answer. She had fallen asleep.

Kaz and Little John watched the rest of the movie with Maddie. When it was over, Maddie turned off the TV. "Claire?" she whispered.

Claire didn't answer. So Maddie draped a blanket over her, then got up to leave. She paused in the doorway.

"Are you ghosts still here?" she whispered, looking around.

"Can we answer her?" Little John asked.

"I guess. She already knows about us. And no one else is here," Kaz said.

"We're . . . still . . . here . . . ," the ghosts wailed at the same time.

Maddie sighed. "Claire's so lucky she has ghost friends to watch over her," she said, leaning against the doorjamb. "I wish I had a ghost friend to watch over me."

"I'll . . . be . . . your . . . ghost . . . friend . . . ," Little John wailed.

"Me . . . too . . . ," Kaz wailed.

"You will? Both of you will?" Maddie grinned. "That's so nice, you guys. Thanks!" Then Maddie turned out the light and went up to her room.

"You already have a solid friend, Kaz," Little John grumbled as they

watched Claire sleep. "You have Claire."

"So?" Kaz said. "You do, too."

"She's more your friend than mine," Little John said. "I want my own solid friend."

"Fine. You can be Maddie's friend," Kaz said.

Little John shook his head. "You already said you'd be her friend, too. I want a solid friend who's all mine."

"Well, maybe one day you'll have one," Kaz said, though he didn't see what the big deal was.

* * * * * * * * * * * * * * * *

In the morning, Maddie came back. "Claire, wake up!" she said, shaking Claire's shoulder.

Claire yawned and stretched. "Did I fall asleep during the movie?"

"Yes," Maddie said. "But you have to

get up now. We have to go to the library."
She wore a yellow T-shirt that said TEEN
ADVISORY BOARD on the front.

"Now?" Claire said, sitting partway
up. "Don't we have to do our schoolwork
first?" She glanced over at Kaz and
Little John. But they didn't know what
Maddie's big hurry was, either.

"Mom said we could go now. The
library needs our help," Maddie said.
"The ghost is back!"

What happened?" Maddie asked as she and Claire moved slowly through the children's center. Kaz and Little John drifted above them. They all stared at the floor in dismay. There were hundreds, maybe even thousands, of books strewn around.

"It looks like there was an earthquake," Claire said.

"This wasn't an earthquake," said Lynette.

"Did someone break into the library?" Maddie asked.

"We don't think so," Andrea replied. "There's no sign of forced entry. Nothing seems to be missing. Nothing is out of place anywhere else in the building. But for some reason, most of the kids' books were on the floor this morning."

A light-haired boy pulled on Claire's

shirt. "It was a ghost," he said. "Probably the same one who was here yesterday."

Little John gasped. "Is he talking about me?" he asked. "Does he think *I* made this mess?"

Kaz remembered that boy from yesterday. He saw Little John. He also said he saw a ghost with chains in the library once.

"It wasn't the ghost from yesterday," said a girl with long braids. She'd been here yesterday, too. She was the one Little John wanted to play with.

"How do you know, Claire?" the light-haired boy asked the girl with the braids.

Kaz, Little John, and Claire all exchanged looks. The girl with the braids was named Claire, too?

"Because he was a nice ghost," Claire-with-the-braids said.

Little John beamed.

"I don't think it was a ghost," Andrea said.

"Don't be too sure about that," Lynette said. "The security guard showed us video footage from last night. We could see books falling off the shelves on the video. But there

wasn't anyone there knocking them off. How do you explain that if it wasn't a ghost?"

"I don't know," Andrea said. "But there's got to be another explanation."

"Maybe whoever did it knew where to stand so they wouldn't get caught on camera?" Claire suggested.

"It's not just all the books on the floor," Lynette said. "The ghost is trying to communicate with us. Look." She pointed at a row of computers.

The same message appeared in large letters on each screen: *Cancel the Halloween party. Or else!* It was signed *The Library Ghost.*

"This is a very dangerous ghost," Lynette said. "We need to cancel this party, and we need to cancel it now. Otherwise there could be trouble."

Maddie looked worried. "We're not going to cancel the party, are we?" she asked Andrea.

Andrea rubbed her forehead. "I don't know yet," she said in a tired voice. "First we need to clean up this mess. Then we'll decide what to do about the party."

"We'll help clean it up. Won't we, Claire?" Maddie said.

"Of course," Claire said. She and Maddie started picking up books.

"Put them in alphabetical order," said a lady who was stacking books on a cart behind them.

"We need to find out who did this," Claire whispered to the ghosts. "I'm going to be busy here for a while. Can you guys go look for clues?"

"C, K, and LJ Detectives to the rescue!" Little John said, punching his fist in the air.

LJ Detectives? Kaz thought with a raised eyebrow. But he wasn't going to argue.

The ghosts wafted past the security guard, who stared intently at all three computer screens in front of her. Kaz circled back to see what was on those screens. It looked like several different views around the library.

"Hurry up, Kaz," Little John called from the dark auditorium.

Kaz swam into the auditorium and followed his brother up over the rows of chairs to the third floor of the library. They floated past the checkout desk and above the escalator that had quit working yesterday. Kaz was glad to see that it was working again today.

"Where are you, you ghost?" Little John called, looking all around.

"We don't know for sure that it's a ghost," Kaz pointed out. "It would take a lot of energy for one ghost to knock all those solid books on the floor. And even more energy to push keys on keyboards and type that warning on all those computer screens."

"If it wasn't a ghost, who was it?" Little John asked.

"Someone who doesn't want the library to have a Halloween party," Kaz replied.

"Like who?" Little John asked.

"I don't know. Maybe Lynette," Kaz said. "You heard her. She was trying to get Andrea to cancel the party."

"You think a *librarian* would knock all those books on the floor?" Little John asked. "Librarians love books."

"Usually," Kaz said.

"I think a ghost did it," Little John said. "Let's go find that dumbwaiter and see if there's a ghost in there today."

"Okay," Kaz said. It was good to consider all possibilities. "I think the dumbwaiter was on the fifth floor."

They swam over to another yellow escalator and followed it up, up, up . . . past a strange cutout in the wall. There

were three large white heads talking inside that wall. For a second, Kaz thought there were ghosts in there. But a sign said it was video art.

When they got to the fifth floor, the ghosts swam over to the dumbwaiter. They shrank a little, then passed through the metal door. But this time there was no dumbwaiter inside. Kaz and Little John were alone inside an empty shaft.

"Where's the dumbwaiter?" Little John asked.

"Shh!" Kaz said. "I hear something."

WAAAAAAAA!

The ghosts looked at each other. "Someone's crying!" Little John said in a low voice.

CHAPTER 8

LOST GHOST

The crying was coming from above them. Kaz and Little John followed the sound up, up, up. They passed headfirst through a metal ceiling and into the bottom shelf of the dumbwaiter compartment. That was where they found a tiny ghost boy sobbing in the corner.

"Aha!" Little John cried. "Found you!"

The ghost boy jumped when he heard Little John's voice. He quickly darted

through the back of the dumbwaiter and disappeared through the wall.

"Little John!" Kaz exclaimed. "You scared him!"

"I didn't mean to," Little John said. "Let's go catch him!"

They passed through the side of the dumbwaiter and looked around.

"Where'd he go?" Kaz asked as he and Little John exp-a-a-a-a-a-nded. They swam to the railing and scanned the living room below.

"There!" Little John pointed. The ghost boy hovered near a purple chair.

"He's fast!" Kaz said. They swam down to the living room.

The other ghost glanced up with alarm, then dived headfirst through the carpet. Kaz and Little John followed him through the second-floor book-sorting

area . . . through the first-floor world-languages area . . . all the way down to a dark parking garage.

When the other ghost swam through the garage floor, Kaz and Little John followed him there, too.

But the garage floor was different from the other floors. It was made of thick, heavy concrete that was hard to swim through.

Kaz couldn't see. He couldn't hear. And he didn't feel like he was getting anywhere. He was starting to feel skizzy. Really skizzy.

He tried to turn around, but he had no idea where he was or how far around he'd turned. He flapped his arms and kicked his legs. He opened his mouth to scream, but nothing came out. If he didn't get out of here soon, he was going to spew!

Finally, Kaz popped back out in the parking garage. He breathed a sigh of relief.

But now he was alone in the parking garage.

* * * * * * * * * * * * * * *

Where was Little John? Where was that other ghost? Did they get through all that concrete? Were they in some underground room?

I better go back into that concrete and look for them, Kaz thought to himself.

He saw a car coming. It was going pretty slow, but still Kaz didn't want it

to drive through him. He shot up to the ceiling and waited for the car to pass below him. Once it did, he floated back down to the floor.

"Here goes nothing," he muttered. He took a deep breath, then dived headfirst back through the concrete. He pumped his arms and kicked his legs, but it was just like before. The concrete was too heavy to swim through. Too thick.

He couldn't do it. He had to turn back. He swam and swam and swam until he was back in the parking garage.

Now what? he wondered, his heart racing.

Surely, Little John would come back. Kaz just had to wait for him.

A bell dinged, and Kaz whirled around. It was the elevator. A solid lady stepped out. She stopped at a booth and

gave a man some money. He stamped
a card and handed it to her. Then she
walked over to a silver car, got in, and
drove away.

Kaz floated around the parking garage,
careful to avoid the ramp that led to the
Outside. He didn't want to blow away
from the library.

He watched people drive into the
garage. And he watched people drive out.

He saw a guy get out of a dirty green
truck near the back wall. *Hey, that guy looks
familiar*, Kaz thought. He watched the
guy walk toward him. It was Bill, the guy
from the fish market! The one who scared
tourists by making that weird fish pop up.

What's he *doing here?* Kaz wondered.
He wished he could follow Bill up into
the library, but he needed to wait for
Little John.

Where *was* Little John? Was he ever coming back?

How long had Kaz been waiting, anyway? What if Claire and Maddie were ready to leave the library? Claire didn't know where Kaz was. What if they left without him and Little John?

Kaz wondered if Little John could hear him. "Little John?" he called. Then he yelled: "LITTLE JOHN!!!"

Nothing.

Kaz waited a little longer. Finally, he decided to go find Claire.

He swam up through the ceiling and came out between the first-floor elevators and the security guard's desk.

Kaz stared. Bill from the fish market was chatting with the security guard! They seemed awfully friendly, smiling and laughing with each other.

"Okay, honey," Bill said. "I'm going to go up to the fifth floor and see if I can get on a computer."

"I'll go find you when I'm finished here," the security guard replied.

Just then, Claire-with-the-braids passed through Kaz. She shivered a little as she and her mom stepped into an elevator.

"Hold the elevator, please," Bill called to them.

Kaz darted out of the way so Bill wouldn't pass through him, too.

"Are you going down?" Claire-with-the-braids' mom asked from inside the elevator.

"Oh. No, I'm going up," Bill said. The next elevator opened. Bill turned and waved goodbye to the security guard as he stepped inside.

Kaz continued into the children's center. All the books were back on the shelves now. And *his* Claire was chatting with some adults near an empty library cart. *Whew*, Kaz thought. *She's still here.*

Claire looked happy to see him, too.

"I need to go to the bathroom," she told the ladies she was talking to. She motioned for Kaz to follow her.

Claire pushed the restroom door open, and Kaz wafted in behind her. She checked all the stalls to make sure there was nobody in them. Once she was sure they were alone, she turned to Kaz. "What happened? You guys were gone a long time." She leaned against the sink. "And where's Little John?"

"I don't know," Kaz moaned. He told Claire how they'd found the sad library ghost in the dumbwaiter and chased him through the library and then through the floor of the parking garage. He told her how hard it was to swim through concrete. How skizzy it made him feel. And he told her how he'd waited and waited for Little John to come back.

"I should never have turned back," Kaz went on. "If I'd kept going all the way through the concrete, I wouldn't have lost Little John."

"You don't know that, Kaz," Claire said. She tried to pat him on the back, but her hand went right through him. "You might have lost him anyway. And you might have lost yourself, too. I think you did the right thing turning back."

Kaz wasn't sure he agreed.

The bathroom door banged open, and Maddie poked her head in. "Claire?" she said. "Are you okay?"

Claire shook her head. "We've got a problem," she said. "Little John is lost."

laire, Maddie, and Kaz took the elevator down to the parking garage. "Where did you last see him?" Claire asked as they walked past the parking attendant. The parking attendant watched them with concern.

"I'll show you," Kaz said, swimming ahead. "It was somewhere around here."

"Is there another level to the parking garage?" Claire asked.

Maddie shook her head. "No. It's just one level."

The parking attendant came out of his booth. "Hey, you kids," he said, walking toward them. "What do you think you're doing down here?"

"We're"—Maddie glanced at Claire—"looking for something we lost."

Claire nodded quickly.

"What did you lose?" the parking attendant asked.

"A book," Claire said at the same time that Maddie said, "Her brother." They looked at each other with surprise.

Now the parking attendant crossed his arms.

"Have you seen anything . . . *strange* down here today?" Claire asked, changing the subject.

"What do you mean by 'strange'?" the parking attendant asked.

"She means ghosts," Maddie said as Claire shifted uncomfortably. "Have you seen any ghosts down here?"

"Oh," the parking attendant said. "Not today. I usually see them when I work

the night shift. They come up through the floor when the library closes."

"They do?" Claire said.

Kaz couldn't tell if the parking attendant was telling the truth or not. The only way this guy would see those ghosts was if they were glowing.

"Where do they come from?" Maddie asked. "What's under here?" She tapped her heel against the floor.

"I don't know," the parking attendant said. "Seattle Public Library Ghost Headquarters? All I know is, they come up when the library closes at night and they go back down when the library reopens the next morning."

How? Kaz wondered. *How do they get through all that concrete?*

* * * * * * * * * * * * * *

"There isn't anything under the library," a reference librarian told Claire and Maddie a few minutes later. His name badge said DAVID.

"Really?" Maddie asked. Kaz hovered above them.

"Really," David said. "This building opened in 2004. It was built on top of the old library, which opened in 1960. And that building was built on top of *another* old library. There have been three different libraries on this same spot. But there's nothing under the library."

"Are you sure?" Claire asked, resting her elbows on the desk. "Maybe there's a secret room left over from one of the old libraries."

"Like in the Underground," Maddie said. "In fact, maybe part of the Underground is under the library!" She

said "*the* Underground" like it was a place you could go.

"No. The Underground is below Pioneer Square," David said. "That's where the original city of Seattle was. Did you know that?"

"No." Claire shook her head.

David leaned back in his chair. "Well, back in the 1800s, the city of Seattle sat quite a bit lower than it does today,"

he explained. "This was a problem because the area was prone to flooding. People who lived up the hill had flush toilets that emptied into the bay. But the toilets often backed up during high tide and spilled sewage into the streets."

"Ew," Claire said as Maddie made a face.

"In 1889, there was a big fire that destroyed much of the city," David went on. "When they rebuilt, they decided to raise the city. There were ladders at all the street corners. You had to go down the ladder to get to the store entrance."

"You mean it was all open? Like a big pit?" Claire said. "Did anyone ever fall in?"

"Seventeen men fell to their deaths," David said. "For a while there were two levels of town. Then in 1907, the bubonic plague hit and the whole lower

level was closed off. It wasn't reopened until the 1960s when people decided to clean up Pioneer Square. *That's* where the Underground is. Under Pioneer Square. You can go down there on a tour and see all the old tunnels and storefronts. It's pretty interesting."

"How do you know part of the Underground isn't under the library, too?" Maddie asked. "Pioneer Square isn't very far from here."

"Because we're on a hill. Pioneer Square is down the hill. It doesn't extend up this far," David said. He studied the girls. "I'm glad you're both interested in Seattle history. But *why* are you so interested? And why are you so concerned about what's under the library?"

Claire and Maddie looked at each other. "The guy in the parking garage said

that ghosts come up into the library from under the floor," Maddie said.

David laughed. "Oh, he's pulling your leg," he said.

But what if he isn't pulling their leg? Kaz wondered. What if he really did see ghosts coming up through the floor? A lot of people have seen and heard ghosts in this library. Ghosts other than me and Little John.

Claire and Maddie stepped away from the reference desk. "What do you think, Claire?" Maddie asked. "Do you think a bunch of ghosts came up through the parking garage and knocked all those books on the floor? Or do you think there's some other explanation?"

"I don't know yet," Claire said. "It's a mystery!"

Maddie pulled out her phone and

checked the display. "Well, it's a mystery we'll have to solve another day," she said. "If we don't get home soon, my mom will freak."

"We can't leave!" Kaz cried as Maddie headed for the door. "What about Little John?"

Claire stopped.

"What?" Maddie said. "What's the matter?"

"Kaz doesn't want to leave without his brother," Claire told Maddie.

"Well, we can't stay. My mom's expecting us," Maddie said.

"Do you want to stay here by yourself tonight and wait for Little John to come back?" Claire asked Kaz.

Kaz shook his head. He absolutely did not want to do that.

"We'll come get you tomorrow," Claire promised. "Plus you could also find out if ghosts really do come up through the floor during the night."

Kaz still didn't want to stay. Not the whole night. Not all by himself.

But what if Little John *did* come back?

"It's your decision, Kaz," Claire said. "Whatever you want to do is fine."

It was a hard choice. In the end, Kaz decided to go with Claire.

We forgot to ask Andrea whether or not she was going to cancel the Halloween party," Claire said. She and Maddie stood on the underground platform waiting for their bus. Kaz hovered inside the water bottle that hung from Claire's shoulder.

"I didn't forget to ask her," Maddie said. "You know how sometimes you want to ask your parents something and you know that if you ask today, they'll

say no. But if you wait until tomorrow, they might say yes?"

Claire nodded.

"That's how I felt about asking Andrea about the Halloween party," Maddie said.

Kaz was so worried about Little John, he'd forgotten all about the Halloween party.

"Tomorrow might be a better day to ask," Maddie said, "as long as nothing else happens at the library tonight."

A bus pulled up, but the girls didn't get on it. Kaz watched it drive away into one of the tunnels.

Wait, Kaz thought, peering into the tunnel. *Where exactly does that tunnel go?* He knew it went under a bunch of downtown buildings. But which ones?

David, the reference librarian, told

Claire and Maddie there wasn't anything under the library. But maybe he meant there weren't any *buildings* under there. Could there be a transit tunnel?

"Hey, Claire!" Kaz called from inside the bottle. "Do you know where these tunnels go?"

If there was a transit tunnel under the library, maybe a ghost could get to it if he swam all the way through the concrete. In which case, Little John might be in one of these tunnels!

"CLAIRE!" Kaz called, louder this time. "WHERE DO THESE TUNNELS GO? DO THEY GO UNDER THE LIBRARY?"

But it had gotten noisy on the platform. Claire couldn't hear Kaz calling to her.

A bus stopped in front of Claire and

Maddie, and this time they got on. They tromped to the back of the bus and plopped down in the middle of the last bench.

Kaz thought about the ghosts that passed through the bus yesterday. If Little John was in the tunnel, maybe *he'd* pass through the bus like those other ghosts did. If he did, Kaz didn't want Little John to miss him. He started to pass through Claire's water bottle.

"What are you doing?" Claire asked.

"I'm not doing anything," Maddie said.

"I didn't mean you," Claire whispered as two ladies in front of them turned to look.

Now that he had Claire's attention, Kaz asked, "Do you know if this tunnel goes under the library? If so, Little

John could be in the tunnel or on a bus."

"I don't know," Claire said. She turned to her cousin. "Do you know if the transit tunnel goes under the library?"

Maddie shrugged. "No idea," she said, pulling out her phone. "But we can look for a map on our phones once we're through the tunnel."

"Can you look now?" Kaz asked. If the tunnel did run under the library, he would quickly get off this bus and go try to find his brother.

Claire shook her head. "We can't get online in the tunnel—only on the underground platform," she said.

Kaz groaned. He could see daylight up ahead. The bus was coming out of the tunnel. He wouldn't be able to get off the bus now.

Claire and Maddie bent over their

phones, searching for a map of the transit tunnels.

"Got it!" Claire said, zooming in with her fingers.

Maddie leaned toward Claire, and Kaz tried to see between them.

"Nope," Maddie said. "They're close. The library's over here." She touched a spot on Claire's phone. "But the transit tunnel is over there. It's, like, half a block away."

So much for that idea.

✳ ✳ ✳ ✳ ✳ ✳ ✳ ✳ ✳ ✳ ✳ ✳ ✳ ✳ ✳ ✳ ✳

That night, Claire and Maddie carved pumpkins. Aunt Beth helped Claire carve a funny face in one of the pumpkins. Maddie used a pattern to poke holes and cut a design in the other one.

Claire couldn't tell what the design

was until Maddie finished. It was a witch on a broomstick with a full moon behind her.

"That looks nice," Claire said.

"Thanks," Maddie said, picking up her pumpkin. "Let's go outside and see how they look in the dark."

Not wanting to be left behind, Kaz shrank down . . . down . . . down . . . and passed through Claire's water bottle. Claire grabbed her bottle and her pumpkin and followed Maddie out onto the front porch.

Maddie lit the candles inside the pumpkins. Then the girls clomped down the steps so they could see them glowing from the sidewalk.

"They look good!" Maddie declared.

"Scary, but not *too* scary," Claire said.

Claire and Maddie sat down on the

bottom step. Claire set her bottle down beside her.

"I hope we can find Little John," Maddie said, stretching out her legs on the sidewalk. "I hope you and Kaz don't have to go back to Iowa without him."

Kaz felt something catch in his throat. He didn't even want to think about that possibility.

"I hope we can find him, too," Claire said. "We've actually got two mysteries to solve. The mystery of who messed up the children's center and the mystery of what happened to Little John. But I have a feeling those two mysteries are related."

"They both involve ghosts," Maddie said.

"Yes," Claire agreed. "So let's start at the beginning." She didn't have her notebook, so she just talked. "You heard

a ghost crying in the library dumbwaiter before I ever got here. We found out there really was a ghost, but we never found out why he was crying."

"Your ghost friends found him and chased him through the floor in the parking garage," Maddie said, picking up the story. "Then one of them got lost, too."

"So if we find the ghost from the dumbwaiter, we'll find Little John," Kaz said.

"Not necessarily," Claire said.

"Not necessarily what?" Maddie asked.

"Kaz thinks that if we find the ghost from the dumbwaiter, we'll find his brother," Claire explained. "But Little John may have lost that ghost somewhere under the parking garage."

Kaz groaned.

"So, what about the mess in the children's center?" Maddie asked. "It could've been ghosts. But I have to tell you, Claire, I've been wondering if Lynette did it."

"Lynette?" Claire looked surprised. "She's a librarian. Why would a librarian throw all those books on the floor?"

Little John said the same thing when Kaz suggested that maybe Lynette did it. Kaz didn't have an answer to that question.

But Maddie did. "Maybe she did it to get Andrea to cancel the Halloween party," she said. "Someone who works at the library might know where to stand so they don't get caught on camera."

"Hmm," Claire said thoughtfully.

"I . . . can . . . think . . . of . . .

another . . . suspect . . . ," Kaz wailed inside the bottle. "Remember . . . that . . . guy . . . from . . . the . . . fish . . . market . . . ? He . . . was . . . in . . . the . . . library . . . today . . ."

Claire picked up the bottle. "Why is he a suspect?" she asked as she and Maddie peered in at Kaz.

"We . . . know . . . he . . . likes . . . to . . . play . . . tricks . . . on . . . people . . . ," Kaz wailed. "Maybe . . . he . . . pushed . . . the . . . books . . . off . . . the . . . shelves . . . with . . . a . . . stick . . ."

"Like how he used that stick to make the weird fish jump up?" Maddie asked.

"Yes . . . ," Kaz wailed.

"How would he know where to stand so he wouldn't be on the video?" Claire asked. "He doesn't work at the library. Plus, wouldn't you see the stick in the video?"

"Depends on the stick," Maddie said.

"The . . . security . . . guard . . . could . . . have . . . told . . . him . . . where . . . to . . . stand . . . ," Kaz wailed. "I . . . saw . . . them . . . talking . . . They . . . acted . . . like . . . boyfriend . . . and . . . girlfriend . . ."

"Really," Maddie said. "That's interesting. Maybe they were in on it together?"

"Why?" Claire asked. "Why would a library security guard and a guy who works at the fish market want to mess up the children's center?"

"I don't know," Maddie said. Kaz didn't know, either.

"But I don't know why a ghost would mess up the children's center, either," Claire said, resting her elbows on her knees.

The girls were quiet for a few minutes, each lost in her own thoughts.

Then Maddie said, "Hey, Claire. If you looked at the video, would you be able to see a ghost on it?"

Claire thought for a minute. "Maybe," she said.

"Then we should go back to the library and ask the security guard to show us the video," Maddie said.

"Good idea," Claire said. "Ghosts or not, maybe we'll see something on the video that everyone else missed."

"Sounds . . . like . . . a . . . plan . . . ," Kaz wailed.

orry," the security guard said to Claire and Maddie the next afternoon. "I can't let you see that video." Rain plunked against the outside windows.

"What? Why not?" Claire asked as Kaz passed through her water bottle and exp-a-a-a-a-nded beside her.

The security guard laughed. "Because you're kids!"

"So?" Maddie said.

"The video is not a toy," the security guard said.

"I'm going to see if Little John came back last night. Okay, Claire?" Kaz said. She nodded slightly.

Now, where would Little John be if he did come back? Kaz wondered. Probably the children's center.

Kaz swam up over the security guard's head and through the glass wall behind her. "Little John?" he called, looking around. "Are you here, Little John?"

Kaz didn't see his brother. He drifted down through the short, slanted wall into the "secret room" that Little John had found yesterday.

No Little John in there, either.

Claire and Maddie were still arguing with the security guard when Kaz passed

back through the wall. He searched the rest of the first floor, then sailed up along the conveyor belt that carried books from the book return to the second floor.

"Little John?" he called again.

But Little John wasn't on the second floor.

Kaz searched the third, fourth, fifth, sixth, seventh, eighth, ninth, tenth, and eleventh floors. He called Little John's name on every single floor.

No luck.

The only place he hadn't checked was the parking garage. Kaz floated down through all the floors, all the way to the parking garage. "Little John?" he called, looking both ways.

Nothing.

Kaz considered passing through the concrete floor. Maybe this time he would

keep going without turning around.

But without knowing for sure whether that would lead to Little John, or *anywhere*, he didn't think he wanted to try it.

He went back up to the main floor to see if Claire and Maddie had managed to talk the security guard into showing them the video. But the security guard was all alone at her table.

Where were Claire and Maddie?

"Over here," Claire called as Kaz started to pass through the glass wall. He was going to search the children's center. But Claire and Maddie were sitting by themselves in the front row of the dark auditorium. They looked as glum as Kaz felt.

"That security guard wouldn't let us look at the video," Claire said.

"We even tried to get Andrea to talk to her, but she wouldn't. Andrea's canceling the Halloween party."

"She is? Did something else happen to make her cancel it?" Kaz asked.

Claire shook her head. "She just said that since a bunch of kids said they

weren't coming now, it made sense to cancel it."

"So, no Halloween party. We don't know what happened to Little John. Plus, it's raining outside," Kaz said. This had turned into a really crummy visit to Seattle.

"I'm really sorry about Little John," Claire said.

"Thanks," Kaz said.

"Hey, I just thought of something," Maddie said, sitting up a little straighter. "People say there are ghosts in the Underground. The Underground tour is only a couple blocks from here. We could walk down there. It's not tourist season, so we could probably get on the next tour. If there's a ghost in there, maybe *he* can help us solve one or both of our mysteries."

"How would a ghost in the Underground

be able to help us?" Kaz asked. "What would he know about ghosts in the library?"

Claire shrugged. "It's worth a try. Unless you've got a better idea?" she asked Kaz.

Kaz didn't. So he shrank down . . . down . . . down and went inside Claire's water bottle.

* * * * * * * * * * * * * * * *

The Underground tour began aboveground, in a building that looked like an old saloon. Claire and Maddie sat on hard wooden benches listening to their tour guide, Wendy, talk about the early settlers. Kaz stayed inside the bottle.

Wendy led the group outside into the rain. Some people put up umbrellas as they tromped across Pioneer Square.

They crossed the street and stopped beside a stairwell.

"Be careful. The stairs might be slippery," Wendy said as she headed down the stairs and unlocked a door. "And if you're tall, watch your head."

Claire and Maddie held the railing as they followed the group down the stairs.

"Oh, wow," Claire said, stepping through the doorway. She went around a tight corner, and her water bottle bumped against a brick wall.

Kaz passed through the bottle and followed Claire along a narrow wooden walkway. There was a lot of junk down here. Rusty old tools. Pieces of wood. Dirt. Rocks. Even a dusty sofa and part of a toilet.

The tour group stopped beside some old pictures of the city and listened to Wendy talk more about Seattle in the late 1800s.

Kaz looked around, but he didn't see any ghosts down here.

Wendy finished her story, then directed the group up some other stairs. Kaz saw the open door just in time to shrink down . . . down . . . down . . . and scurry back inside Claire's bottle.

Was the tour over?

No. Once everyone was out in the alley, Wendy went around a corner and

pointed out a section of sidewalk that had a bunch of purple squares in it. "Take a good look at these purple squares as you walk over them," she said.

Claire and Maddie walked over the squares, then followed the people in front of them down more stairs into another part of the Underground.

It was brighter here than it was in the other section. Outside light filtered in through windows in the ceiling. Green plants grew through the dirt around the windows and hung down into the room.

"Do those windows look familiar?" Wendy pointed at the ceiling.

Everyone looked up. "Is that where we were standing outside?" one of the dads asked. He held a little boy on his shoulders.

"It is," Wendy said. "Do you recognize the squares?"

Kaz passed through Claire's water bottle to get a closer look.

"Hey, who are you?" said a ghostly voice.

Kaz and Claire both whirled around.

A ghost with a set of chains hovered in a curved brick entryway behind them.

137

CHAPTER 12

NO SOLIDS ALLOWED

'm Kaz. Who are you?"

"Howard," the other ghost replied. He looked older than Mom and Pops, but not as old as Grandmom and Grandpop.

"I want to show you how much light comes through those squares in the ceiling," Wendy told the tour group. "Does anyone mind if I turn out the lights? No one here is afraid of ghosts?"

"WOOOOOOO!" several college

students said from the back of the group.

Howard rolled his eyes.

Wendy went around a corner and flipped a switch. The light went out, but the tunnel was still as light as it was before Wendy flipped the switch.

"Huh. Look at that." The solid people looked around in amazement.

Wendy turned the light back on, then launched into another story about old Seattle. *How many stories does she have, anyway?* Kaz wondered.

"Where'd you come from, Kaz?" Howard asked. "I don't think I've seen you down here before."

"I came with her." Kaz pointed to Claire, who nodded slightly at Howard.

"You came with a solid girl," Howard said. "Can she see us?"

"Yes," Kaz replied.

Howard peered at Claire with suspicion. "Is she a ghost hunter?"

"More like a ghost *helper*," Kaz said. "Her name's Claire. She's my friend." Kaz gave Howard a brief history of his relationship with Claire. Then, as the

tour group moved to a new part of the tunnel, he told him how Little John had gotten lost when they followed a sad ghost boy through the floor in the library parking garage.

"You haven't, by any chance, seen my brother, have you?" Kaz asked. "Or the other ghost?"

"Not in the last day or two. I haven't seen any ghost kids who were on their own since last week. Well, except for you," Howard said, his chains rattling as he drifted beside Kaz.

But Kaz wasn't really on his own. He had Claire.

Kaz took a closer look at the chains in Howard's hands. "Hey, why do you have those chains?" he asked.

Howard grinned. "I like to mess with the tour groups that come down here.

Watch this." He waited for most of the group to walk past them. Maddie stayed with the group, but Claire hung back by the ghosts.

"What?" Kaz asked Howard. "What are you going to do?"

Howard swam up behind some college students at the back of the line. "Look . . . behind . . . you . . . ," he wailed softly.

When two of them turned to look, Howard glowed. He made the chains glow, too, as he rattled them.

"AAAHHHHHHH!" one of the students shrieked.

Claire covered her mouth.

Howard quickly stopped glowing before Maddie and a bunch of other people turned around.

"Did you see that? What *was* that?

I don't know!" The college students talked over one another.

"I warned you about the ghosts," Wendy said from the front of the group. "Let's keep moving, please."

Maddie let the rest of the group walk past her while she waited for Claire to catch up.

"Have you ever done that in the Seattle Public Library?" Kaz asked Howard as they followed Claire. He remembered the light-haired boy who said he'd seen a ghost with chains.

"Sometimes," Howard admitted.

"You mean you *can* get to the library from here?" Kaz said. "Through the tunnels?"

"Of course," Howard said. He seemed surprised that Kaz didn't know that.

"What's happening?" Maddie asked Claire.

Claire put her finger to her lips.

"How? The librarian told us there aren't any tunnels under the library," Kaz said to Howard.

Howard laughed. "The librarian is wrong," he said. "There are all kinds of tunnels under the city. The solid people know about some of those tunnels, but not *all* of them. There are a lot of tunnels that only the underground ghosts know about."

So maybe Little John and that other ghost are somewhere in this underground tunnel system, Kaz thought. "Can you show Claire and me how to get to the library?" he asked. Maybe they'd find Little John along the way.

Howard turned and looked behind

him. "Well . . . I don't want to miss the next tour group," he said. "But I'll tell you how to get there. First, go back to that last room. Find the door that says BANK VAULT and pass through it. There's a tunnel in there. Follow it until it splits in two, then go right. At the next split, turn left. The tunnel will get a lot smaller. When it turns a corner, you're below the library. Easy-peasy. But your solid friend can't go with you. No solids allowed in *those* tunnels. They're dangerous for solid people."

Kaz gulped. He wasn't sure he wanted to go by himself.

"Excuse me!" Wendy said sharply. She walked through Howard and stopped beside Claire and Maddie. "You two have to stay with the group."

"Sorry. We're coming," Claire said as she and Maddie started walking.

Satisfied, Wendy hurried to the front of the group. Claire and Maddie slowed down.

"Are you going to tell me what's happening?" Maddie asked Claire. "Is there another ghost down here?"

Claire nodded slightly.

"Does he know Kaz's brother?" Maddie asked.

"No," Claire said. "But he knows the way to the library. He just told Kaz how to get there through a bunch of tunnels that only the underground ghosts know about! Little John and that other ghost could be somewhere in one of those tunnels." She turned to Kaz. "You're going to have to go check it out."

"But . . . I don't want to go by myself," Kaz said.

"You have to," Claire said. "I can't pass through walls, and I can't go in those tunnels."

Claire was right. Kaz had to go alone. There was no other choice.

"Good luck," Claire said. "We'll meet you back at the library."

* * * * * * * * * * * * * * *

Right, then left, then up into the library, Kaz repeated Howard's directions to himself as he passed through a gritty cobweb.

There were no windows or lightbulbs in the ceiling in this part of the Underground. Some of the boards around the doorways were cracked and broken. And there were places where the ceiling had caved in. But he kept going. He floated through cobweb after cobweb. He didn't like this. He didn't like it at all.

All of a sudden, he heard laughter. Ghostly laughter.

"Hello?" Kaz called.

"Hello," a ghostly voice called back.

Kaz could see the ghosts up ahead now. There were three of them. Two men and a lady. They hovered in midair, right near a bend in the tunnel. They were laughing at something just around the corner.

"What's so funny?" Kaz asked as he wafted up behind them.

The lady ghost pointed. "Ghost hunters," she said. Which made the other ghosts laugh even harder.

Kaz saw two solid men partway down the tunnel. There were bright lights on their helmets. Big headphones covered their ears. One of the men held a strange-looking gadget that beeped. The other held a black box. They stared very seriously at the dirt wall in front of them.

"I didn't think solid people were allowed in these tunnels," Kaz said.

"They're not," said one of the ghost men. "But those two sneaked down, anyway."

"What do you suppose they see?" asked the ghost lady.

"Nothing," one of the ghost men replied. And they all laughed.

"Um, do you guys know the way to the library?" Kaz asked the ghosts. "Is it that way?" He pointed a shaky finger at the ghost hunters.

"Yes," the ghost lady replied. "But don't worry about them. They'll never know you're there."

She was probably right. If she was wrong, and somehow those ghost hunters managed to catch Kaz and put him in their black box, he could probably pass through the side and escape.

Kaz took a deep breath and continued down the tunnel. Toward the ghost hunters.

"Go through them! Go through them!" the ghosts behind him urged.

Kaz let his left foot dangle through the head of one of the ghost hunters as he sailed above them. The ghosts behind him laughed and laughed.

Even Kaz couldn't help smiling a little bit. The "ghost hunters" hadn't noticed him at all.

Kaz kept going. At the next split, he took the left tunnel. This ceiling was a lot lower, just like Howard had said it would be. The whole tunnel was getting smaller and narrower. Kaz had to shrink a little to fit through it.

All of a sudden, he stopped. He heard something. It sounded like ghostly crying.

CHAPTER 13

DO WE HAVE A DEAL?

Kaz followed the tunnel around a corner. There, in front of him, was the very same ghost boy that he and Little John had chased through the library yesterday.

Unfortunately, Little John wasn't with him.

The ghost boy hugged his knees to his chest and sobbed.

"Hello?" Kaz said gently. He didn't want to scare the boy the way Little John had.

The boy stopped crying for a second. He looked up at Kaz, and his eyes widened. He started to swim away.

"Wait!" Kaz said, wafting after him. "Don't go. Please don't go."

Surprisingly enough, the boy stopped.

Kaz drifted a little closer. "What's your name?" he said. "My name's Kaz."

"Oliver," the boy said.

"Hi, Oliver," Kaz said. "Why are you crying?"

Oliver wiped the back of his hand across his face. "I got blown away," he said with a sniff.

"Oh no," Kaz said. "From where? Where's your haunt?"

Oliver shrugged.

"How did you get blown away?" Kaz asked.

Oliver shrugged again. "It was an accident," he said.

Kaz felt bad for Oliver. "I got separated from my family once, too," he said. "We used to live in this old schoolhouse, but it got torn down and then the wind blew us to different places. But guess what? I found my whole family again!"

Now Oliver looked at him with interest.

"Unfortunately, I lost my little

154

brother yesterday," Kaz went on. "Do you know where he is? The last time I saw him, well . . . we were chasing you."

"That wasn't very nice of you," Oliver said in a small voice.

"We weren't trying to be mean," Kaz said. "We wanted to know why you were crying. We wanted to help."

"How did you find your family when you got lost?" Oliver asked.

"A solid girl helped me," Kaz said. He expected Oliver to have questions about that. Whenever Kaz told another ghost about Claire, the ghost always had lots of questions.

But the only thing Oliver wanted to know about Claire was, "Can she help me find *my* family?"

"Maybe," Kaz replied. "Probably.

But we're leaving in a couple of days and—"

"I know what happened to your brother," Oliver interrupted. He sniffed again. "I'll tell you . . . *if* your solid friend can find my family. But she has to help me first. Deal?" He held out his hand.

What if Claire can't find Oliver's family? Kaz wondered.

Well, he didn't have any other options. So he shook Oliver's hand and said, "Deal."

"Where's your solid friend right now?" Oliver asked.

"Her name is Claire," Kaz said. "She was at the Underground, but she's meeting me in the library. Do you know how to get to the library? Do we just swim up through the ceiling?"

"Pretty much," Oliver said. "It takes a while, though. Hold your breath and kick as hard as you can. Eventually you'll come out in the parking garage."

Oliver took a deep breath and swam up through the dirt ceiling.

Kaz did the same thing.

Deep breath . . . then kick, kick, kick, kick, kick through the concrete . . . kick, kick, kick, kick, kick . . . kick, kick, kick, kick, kick . . . oh, how Kaz hated concrete. He was starting to feel skizzy again.

But if a little kid ghost like Oliver could swim through it, so could Kaz.

Kick, kick, kick, *pop!* He was in the parking garage.

Oliver was, too.

"Okay. Where's your friend?" Oliver asked as a solid car drove through him.

Kaz darted out of the way so the car wouldn't drive through *him*, too. "We'll meet her and her cousin upstairs," he said. They hadn't actually agreed on a meeting spot. But Kaz had a feeling Claire and Maddie would go to the children's center.

The ghosts swam up through the ceiling. The ceiling seemed to go on longer than it should, until Kaz realized he was passing through a shelf of books behind the checkout desk. He veered to

the side and led Oliver past the elevators, past the security guard, and through the glass wall into the children's center.

Kaz looked around. He didn't see Claire or Maddie. "They'll be here soon," Kaz told Oliver.

The ghosts drifted around the children's center.

"Did you come here two nights ago and knock a bunch of books on the floor and leave a message on all the computers that said 'cancel the Halloween party or else'?" Kaz asked.

"That wasn't just me," Oliver said right away. "Lots of ghosts helped with that."

So it *was* ghosts. There was one mystery solved.

"Why?" Kaz asked. "Why would you do all that?"

"We don't want all those solid kids to

stay the whole night," Oliver said. "The library is supposed to be *ours* at night. Ghosts get the library at night. Solid people get it during the day. That's the deal."

"What deal?" Kaz asked.

"The deal that the solids and the ghosts made," Oliver said.

"What solids? What ghosts?" Kaz wanted to know. And what was it with Oliver and deals, anyway?

"I don't know," Oliver said. "The deal was made a long, long, long time ago. And now those solids are breaking the deal. It's not fair. We want them to know it's not fair. That's why we knocked all the books on the floor."

"Oh," Kaz said. He didn't know what else to say. He wondered if Maddie and the others knew about this deal. Not that it mattered. The party was canceled. The

ghosts would have the library to themselves on Halloween.

"What about when the escalators stopped working?" Kaz asked. "Did you or the other ghosts make that happen?"

"No," Oliver said. "But I bet those solid people *think* we did. Solid people always blame ghosts when stuff like that happens."

"True," Kaz said. "Lots of solid people say they don't believe in ghosts, yet when something happens that they can't explain, they think ghosts did it."

"Are you sure your solid friend is coming?" Oliver asked.

"Yes," Kaz said. But it had been a while since they'd separated in the Underground. Kaz had managed to get all the way through the secret underground tunnels into the library. Shouldn't Claire and Maddie have been back by now, too?

CHAPTER 14

GONE FOR GOOD

Maybe they're in a different part of the library," Kaz said. "Let's go look for them." He started to pass through the glass wall when, *finally*, he saw Claire and Maddie walking into the library.

"There they are," he said. "Over here, Claire!" He waved.

Claire smiled. "We need a private place to talk," she told Maddie in a quiet voice as she stomped the rain from her

feet. "Kaz is back. And there's another ghost boy with him. But it's not Little John or the ghost from the Underground. Should we go in one of the bathrooms?"

"You want to take boy ghosts into the girls' bathroom?" Maddie shrieked.

A couple of girls turned to look at Maddie and Claire.

Maddie's face reddened. She probably realized how that sounded. She leaned close to Claire and said, "I know where we can talk," she said. "Follow me."

She led Claire and the ghosts up the escalator to the third floor. They went over to the teen area, past some bookshelves, and over to a black tape that stretched from the wall to a pillar. Maddie ducked under it.

"Are we allowed back there?" Claire asked.

"Yes. This is the teen work room," Maddie said. "It's where teen volunteers go to work on projects."

Claire ducked under the tape. Kaz and Oliver sailed over it. And now they were in a small room with a table and chairs and a row of cabinets.

"There are librarians back there," Maddie said, pointing to another door they could sort of see through next to the cabinets. "We should talk softly."

Claire nodded. "That means you guys shouldn't wail," she said to the ghosts.

"You'll tell me everything the ghosts say, though. Won't you?" Maddie asked.

"Of course," Claire said. She sat down at the table. "So, who's your friend, Kaz?"

"His name's Oliver," Kaz said, wafting

closer. "Oliver, this is Claire and Maddie."

"Hi, Oliver," Claire said, waving at him. Oliver waved back.

"Claire can see and hear you, but Maddie can't," Kaz told Oliver. "Claire, Oliver is the ghost who's been crying in the dumbwaiter. He got separated from his family. That's why he was crying. He knows where Little John is, but he wants you to help him find his family before he'll tell us about Little John."

Claire repeated all of that for Maddie.

Kaz also told Claire about the deal that some solid people and ghost people made about the library a long time ago and how that was why the ghosts had messed up the children's center.

Claire repeated *that* for Maddie, too.

"So now we know who's been haunting the library and why," Maddie

said. "But we can't do anything about it. The party's already canceled."

"How many ghosts are in your family?" Claire asked Oliver. "And where did you last see them?"

"There are five ghosts in my family," Oliver said. "My mom, my dad, my brother, Owen, my sister, Olivia, and me. I last saw them at home, before I accidentally passed through the wall."

"You mean we just have to take you home and then you'll be with your family?" Claire said. "That's easy. Where do you live?"

"In the castle by the sky church," Oliver said.

Claire turned to Maddie. "He lives in the castle by the sky church. What's that?"

"No idea," Maddie replied.

"It's a big, big screen that plays music videos," Oliver said, stretching his arms wide. "There's a huge pile of instruments, mostly guitars, that goes from the floor to the big, high ceiling. You can watch movies about outer space and play video games. Lots of solid people come to visit, too. Our haunt is kind of a museum."

Claire repeated that for Maddie.

"Oh, he probably lives at the MoPOP," Maddie said.

"What's the MoPOP?" Kaz asked.

"It's a museum that has music and science-fiction stuff," Claire replied.

"Yeah . . . that's . . . where . . . I . . . live . . . !" Oliver wailed. He was so excited that he started to glow.

Maddie laughed. "Well, let's take you home, Oliver!"

"I thought you said that girl couldn't see or hear us," Oliver said, pointing at Maddie.

"You're glowing," Kaz said, trying not to feel jealous.

"I am?" Oliver looked down at himself. "Hey, I *am*! I didn't know I could glow." He beamed with pride.

Kaz sighed. *Everyone* could glow. Everyone except him.

"We have to shrink so we can fit in Claire's water bottle," Kaz told Oliver. "That's how we'll travel to your haunt."

Kaz thought Oliver would have some questions about traveling inside a solid girl's water bottle. But he shrank down . . . down . . . down . . . and passed through the bottle like he knew exactly what to do.

So Kaz did, too.

Then Claire and Maddie headed out into the rain.

* * * * * * * * * * * * * *

The MoPOP was an even weirder-looking building than the library. From inside Claire's water bottle, it looked like a spaceship. Part of it was light blue. Part of it was silver—or was it gold? It seemed to change color, depending on how close

you were to it. A train track in the sky ran right through the middle.

"That's where I live!" Oliver said, bobbing up and down inside the bottle.

Kaz grabbed him by the arm. "Don't get too excited. If you pass through Claire's water bottle before we get inside, you'll blow away."

Oliver tried to calm himself down. Claire and Maddie went inside the museum and paid admission.

"Okay, now it's safe to pass through," Kaz said. He and Oliver passed through the bottle and exp-a-a-a-a-a-nded.

The lady at the ticket counter gave Claire and Maddie a map of all the exhibits.

"Mom! Dad! I'm home!" Oliver yelled. But there was loud music playing around the corner, so Kaz wasn't sure Oliver's family could hear him.

Oliver went over to a big wooden door and passed through it. Apparently it was heavy, because Maddie and Claire had to work together to pull it open.

Kaz followed the girls into what looked like an enchanted forest. There was a shiny castle to the right. A ghost lady around his mom's age passed through the castle wall near the ceiling. "Oliver?" she said, her eyes wide with disbelief.

A ghost man around Pops's age passed through behind her. "Is that you, son?"

"Mom! Dad!" Oliver cried as he swam to his parents and hugged them.

"What?" Maddie asked Claire. "Why are you smiling like that? Is his family here?"

"Yes," Claire said.

Oliver introduced his parents to Kaz,

Claire, and Maddie. "That one can't see or hear us." He pointed to Maddie. "But the other one can. They brought me home!"

"You got help from solid girls?" Oliver's mom asked.

"Yes!" Oliver said. He told his parents all about Kaz and Claire and what it was like to travel inside a water bottle.

Kaz wanted to interrupt him and ask about Little John, but he remembered how he felt when he saw each of his family members again. He could give Oliver a little time.

"Where are Owen and Olivia?" Oliver asked.

"Probably watching music videos," his pops said. "Let's go see if we can find them." Oliver and his parents passed through the big, heavy door.

Trying to be patient, Kaz followed Oliver and his parents. They went into a huge, LOUD room with a ginormous screen. That screen was taller than their whole library back home.

"Oh, this is the sky church," Maddie said as she and Claire walked in behind the ghosts. "See? It says so right here on the map."

Two teenage ghosts, a boy and a girl, hovered above them, watching the booming videos.

"Owen? Olivia?" Oliver said.

The other ghosts turned. "Oliver?" said the girl.

"You're back!" said the boy.

Then it started all over again: the hugging, the introductions, the explanation of how Oliver had found his way back.

Kaz was out of patience. "You said you'd tell me where Little John was if Claire found your family," he said, wafting over. "She found your family, so . . . where's my brother?"

"Oh. He went with the solid girl," Oliver said like it was no big deal.

Kaz was confused. "What solid girl?"

"The one at the library," Oliver said.

"Okay, why don't you start at the beginning," Kaz said, crossing his arms. "Tell me what happened when Little John chased you through the floor in the parking garage."

"He caught me," Oliver said as his family gathered around. "He told me about you and Claire. He said you'd help me find my family. We went back up into the library and looked for you guys, but we couldn't find you. So we went back to the garage and he left with the solid girl. He said he always wanted his own solid friend."

His own solid friend? Uh-oh. Kaz had heard Little John say that, too. Had Little John made friends with a solid girl like he had made friends with Claire? Was Little John gone for good?

CHAPTER 15

HALLOWEEN IN SEATTLE

Oliver didn't know much about the solid girl that Little John had left with, just that she was around Little John's age. And she carried a water bottle. That was how Oliver knew about water bottles. He'd seen Little John travel in one.

"Attention!" a voice came over the intercom. "The museum will be closing in five minutes."

"We have to go," Maddie said.

"Thanks for bringing my boy home," Oliver's mom said.

Kaz shrank down . . . down . . . down and went inside Claire's bottle. Claire and Maddie walked back to the bus tunnel in the dark and the rain.

What was Kaz going to do? There had to be millions of girls in Seattle. How would he ever find the one that Little John had gone with? And even if he did find her and Little John, would Little John come with him?

How would Kaz ever explain all this to Mom and Pops?

* * * * * * * * * * * * * * *

That night, Claire and Maddie put the finishing touches on their Halloween costumes. Claire was going as a mermaid. Maddie would be a punk rocker. Since there wasn't going to be a party at the

library on Halloween, Maddie said she'd take Claire trick-or-treating instead.

Kaz hovered glumly in the corner.

"Maddie, your phone's ringing!" Aunt Beth called from the kitchen.

Maddie raced out of the room. "Coming," she called.

"Cheer up, Kaz," Claire said. "We don't know for sure that Little John is gone for good. We'll go back to the library one more time tomorrow before trick-or-treating. Maybe he'll be there."

Kaz doubted it. "Little John said he always wanted his own solid friend," he told Claire. "It sounds like he found one."

Maddie rushed back in.

"Well, here's some good news," she said. "That was Andrea on the phone. She called all the kids who signed up for the Halloween party to let them know the party was canceled, and a bunch of moms got upset! When they heard there weren't enough kids signed up, they got a bunch *more* kids to sign up. So the party is back on!"

"For real?" Claire said.

"For real," Maddie said. "We get to skip our schoolwork again tomorrow morning so we can go to the library and help Andrea set up."

"What about the underground ghosts?" Kaz said. When he remembered that Maddie couldn't hear him, he wailed, "What . . . about . . . the . . . underground . . . ghosts . . . ? They . . . won't . . . be . . . happy . . . Solid . . . people . . . aren't . . .

supposed . . . to . . . be . . . in . . . the . . . library . . . at . . . night . . ."

Claire and Maddie looked at each other.

"It's only one night," Maddie said. "Can't we be in the library one night without a bunch of ghosts getting upset?"

"What if we invite the ghosts to come to the party, too?" Claire suggested.

"Oh, I like that," Maddie said. "*Real* ghosts at a Halloween party!"

"How . . . will . . . you . . . invite . . . them . . . ?" Kaz wailed. "How . . . will . . . they . . . know . . . we . . . want . . . them . . . to . . . stay . . . ?"

"We'll put up a big sign that says GHOSTS WELCOME!" Claire said.

Maddie grinned. "People will think we're talking about costumes, not real ghosts." Then her face clouded. "Oh, but what if some of the kids are scared of the ghosts?"

Claire shrugged. "It's Halloween. You've got to expect a ghost or two to show up on Halloween."

* * * * * * * * * * * * *

The next morning Kaz went to the library with Claire and Maddie. While they helped Andrea decorate and get set up for the party, Kaz searched all eleven floors of the library one more time.

Little John was nowhere to be found.

The party was going to be held in the tenth-floor reading room. Kaz watched Claire and Maddie move chairs and tables away from the carpeted area. Next they set up tables for food and games. Then they painted large signs that said: WELCOME TO THE SPL HALLOWEEN PARTY! REAL LIVE GHOSTS WELCOME, TOO!

Kaz watched his solid friends hang

their signs on the tenth floor, outside the children's center on the first floor, and down in the parking garage.

The parking attendant raised an eyebrow. "You two know you're asking for trouble putting up a sign like that, don't you?" he said.

"We don't care. It's Halloween!" Maddie said.

Maddie and Claire were really excited about the party, but Kaz wasn't. It's hard to get excited about a party when you're not sure you'll ever see your little brother again.

* * * * * * * * * * * * * *

Kids started arriving for the party a little before seven. They came dressed as pirates, vampires, skeletons, characters from popular children's books, even a ghost. The one who was dressed like

a ghost had put a white sheet over his head. *He doesn't look anything like a real ghost*, Kaz thought.

The real ghosts started to arrive, too. One by one they drifted slowly up through the floors. "Is it true?" a lady ghost asked Kaz. "Are we really invited to this party?"

Claire adjusted her mermaid costume and walked over. "Yes!" she said to the ghosts. "Welcome! This party is for ghost people *and* solid people!"

"Hooray!" said the ghosts. They came up through the floor, the elevator shaft, and the open part of the library. There seemed to be more ghosts than solid people at this party.

But the one ghost Kaz most wanted to see *wasn't* there.

"I'm glad we decided to go ahead with the party," Andrea said as she helped

Maddie pour glasses of punch. She was dressed as a cat.

"Me too," Maddie replied. "Hey, where's Lynette?"

"I told her she could take the night off," Andrea said. "She doesn't like big parties. And I think you and I and all the teen advisory board members have it covered."

"I think so, too," Maddie said.

The elevator dinged, and a girl skeleton walked out. It was Claire-with-the-braids. She held a water bottle in her hands.

Kaz stared at the water bottle. Was there someone inside?

"Hi, Kaz," Little John said as he passed through the water bottle.

"Little John!" Kaz exclaimed. "You're back! You're really back."

"Wow, Kaz! Look at you!" Little John gaped.

Maddie pulled on Claire's arm. "That's your other ghost friend, isn't it?" she said.

Claire nodded as she grinned at Kaz. In fact, *all* the solid people in the room were looking at Kaz. They were looking at him as though they could actually see him.

Kaz looked down at himself and gasped. "I'm glowing!" But he had no idea how or why he was doing it.

This had happened to him once before. Claire had taken him and his family to visit Grandmom and Grandpop at the nursing home, and Petey, the bird who lived there, squawked and scared him. Kaz had thought glowing had something to do with being scared. But he wasn't scared now. He was happy. Happy to see his brother.

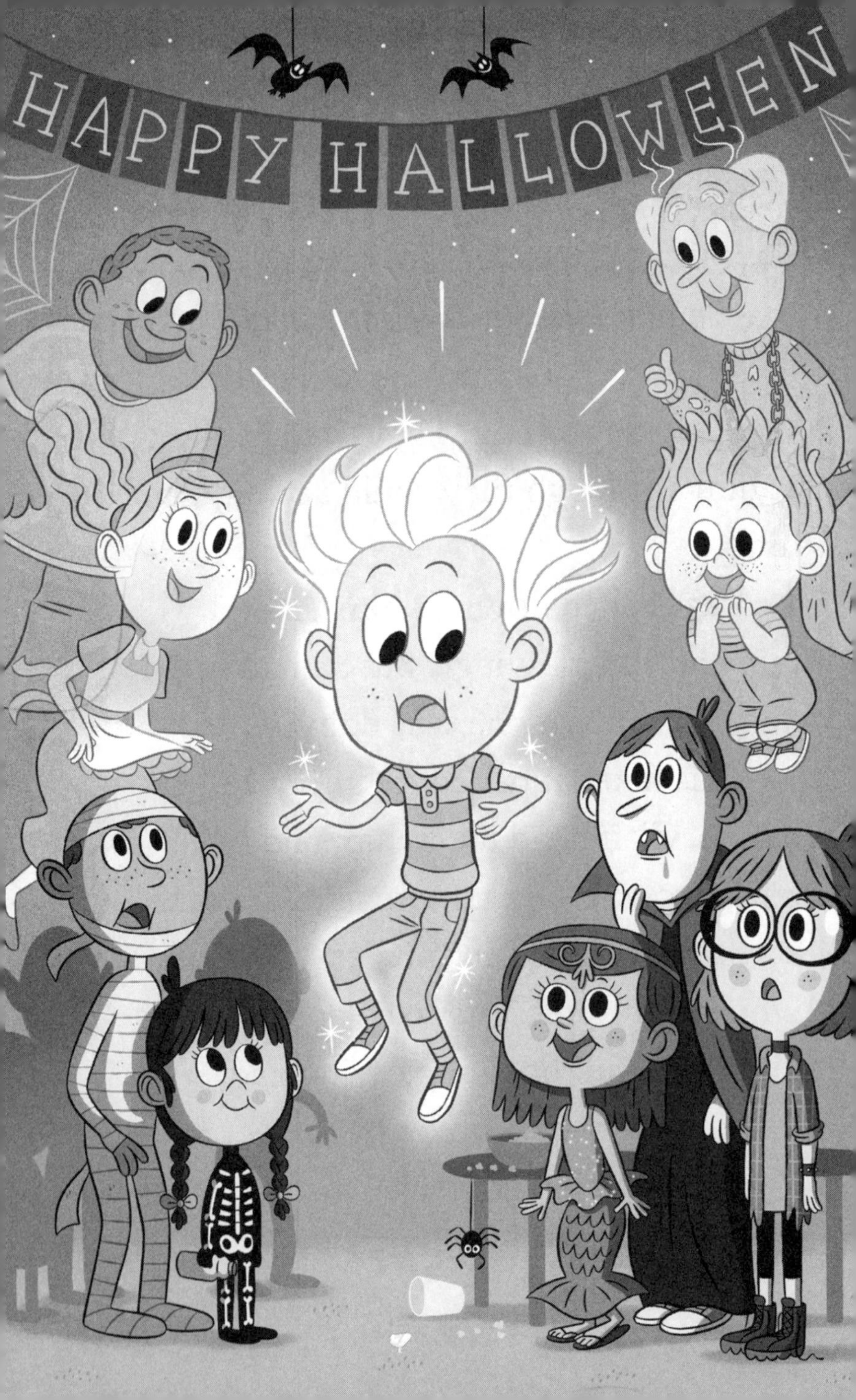
HAPPY HALLOWEEN

"Yay, Kaz!" Little John exclaimed as Kaz's glow started to fade.

Kaz took a deep breath and willed that glow to come back.

It did! Kaz felt a glow bubbling up inside his body and flowing out through his skin. It was like moving an arm . . . shrinking . . . expanding . . . he could do it now. He could glow.

And everyone could see him glowing. He quickly stopped.

"What *was* that?" a girl dressed as a pirate asked. She stared, but she couldn't see Kaz anymore.

"Just one of your friendly neighborhood library ghosts," Maddie said.

The pirate looked a little worried, like she wasn't sure whether or not to believe Maddie.

"Don't worry, Tasha," Claire-with-the-

braids said. "She said *friendly*. All the ghosts in the library are friendly."

Kaz wondered whether Claire-with-the-braids had any idea just how many ghosts there were in the library. His Claire knew how many there were. She could see them. But Claire-with-the-braids could only see them when they glowed.

All of a sudden, Claire-with-the-braids looked worried. "Where are you, Little John?" she asked. She peered into her water bottle. "Are you still in there?"

"No . . . ," Little John wailed. "I'm . . . over . . . here . . . ." He glowed and waved at her.

Now all the solid people were staring in disbelief at Little John.

Claire-with-the-braids grinned and waved back.

Kaz's Claire went to introduce herself to Claire-with-the-braids. While they were getting acquainted, Kaz led Little John away from the crowd.

"Where have you been?" Kaz asked. "What were you thinking, going home with a solid girl! Do you have any idea how worried I've been?"

"You sound like Mom and Pops," Little John said.

"Do you have any idea what Mom and Pops would have said if I'd gone home without you?" Kaz asked.

"Why would you go home without me?" Little John asked.

"BECAUSE I THOUGHT YOU WERE LOST!" Kaz shrieked.

"I wasn't lost," Little John said. "I thought *you* were lost. I looked all over for you. When I couldn't find you,

I decided to go home with *my* friend, Claire."

"Just like that?" Kaz asked. "What if your friend Claire hadn't come tonight? You might never have seen your family again. We could've been separated forever."

"I knew she was coming tonight," Little John said. "I watched her sign up for the party!" He didn't know that Andrea had actually canceled the party. If the party had stayed canceled, Little John would never have found his way back to Kaz.

But he *had* found his way back. That was what was important, Kaz realized.

"You are coming back home with me and Claire, aren't you, Little John?" Kaz asked.

"Yes," Little John replied. "But I want

to come back and visit my Claire. Do you think we can do that?"

"Of course you can do that," Claire said, walking up behind them. Claire-with-the-braids was right beside her.

Claire put her arm around Claire-with-the-braids. "Claire and I are going to keep in touch," she said. "I'll come back to visit Maddie and Aunt Beth. You and Kaz can come, too. And you can go stay with Claire sometimes if you want, Little John."

Claire-with-the-braids nodded eagerly.

A girl behind them looked at them curiously. "Who are you guys talking to?" she asked.

"Our ghost friends," Claire-with-the-braids said, as though it was obvious.

The other girl narrowed her eyes. "Are there *really* ghosts in here?" she asked. "I thought it was a trick."

Kaz's Claire shrugged. "Maybe it's a trick, maybe it's not," she said. "Do you really want to know?"

"No. Not really," the girl said as she skipped away.

"Happy Halloween, Kaz," Claire said, raising her hand.

Kaz touched his ghostly hand to her solid hand. "Happy . . . Halloween . . . Claire . . . ," he wailed.